MYSTERY AT THE MUSEUM

"These guys ate a *lot* of leaves and twigs," Maya said with a grin. "Anyway, Bruno's not our only dinosaur. Over there is an ornithopod footprint in a cast that you can touch. Ornithopods were small-to-medium-size herbivores that mostly ran on two feet. And near that is some fossilized dinosaur poop."

"Ewwwwww!" everyone groaned.

"I'm totally taking a picture of that," Phil said, reaching into his pocket for his cell phone. "Hey, Frank, do you know if—"

"Frank! Look out!" Joe yelled suddenly.

Frank turned—but not in time. He saw a dark flash of wings before something slammed into his face.

THE HARDY BOYS®

SECRET FILES #14

 Fossil Frenzy

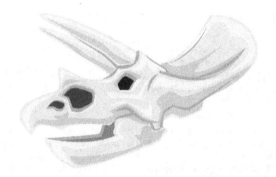

BY **FRANKLIN W. DIXON**

ILLUSTRATED BY **SCOTT BURROUGHS**

ALADDIN · NEW YORK LONDON TORONTO SYDNEY NEW DELHI

This book is a work of fiction. Any references to historical events, real people, or real places are used fictitiously. Other names, characters, places, and events are products of the author's imagination, and any resemblance to actual events or places or persons, living or dead, is entirely coincidental.

 ALADDIN

An imprint of Simon & Schuster Children's Publishing Division
1230 Avenue of the Americas, New York, NY 10020
First Aladdin paperback edition April 2014
Text copyright © 2014 by Simon & Schuster, Inc.
Illustrations copyright © 2014 by Scott Burroughs
Series design by Lisa Vega
Cover design by Jeanine Henderson
All rights reserved, including the right of reproduction in whole or in part in any form.
ALADDIN is a trademark of Simon & Schuster, Inc., and related logo is a registered trademark of Simon & Schuster, Inc.
THE HARDY BOYS is a registered trademark of Simon & Schuster, Inc.
For information about special discounts for bulk purchases, please contact Simon & Schuster Special Sales at 1-866-506-1949 or business@simonandschuster.com.
The Simon & Schuster Speakers Bureau can bring authors to your live event. For more information or to book an event contact the Simon & Schuster Speakers Bureau at 1-866-248-3049 or visit our website at www.simonspeakers.com.
The text of this book was set in Garamond.
Manufactured in the United States of America 1116 QVE
10 9 8 7 6 5 4 3
Library of Congress Control Number 2013955119
ISBN 978-1-4424-9043-7
ISBN 978-1-4424-9044-4 (eBook)

CONTENTS

1

Bad News

Joe Hardy's clawlike fingers crept across the kitchen table and grabbed the helpless hot dog.

"*Roar!*" he growled in his best dinosaur voice. He chomped down on the hot dog with his teeth and tore a piece off.

His brother, Frank, raised his eyebrows. "Uh, what are you supposed to be, exactly?"

"An ultrasaurus. Can't you tell?" Joe said.

"Ultrasauruses are herbivores, remember? They only eat plants," Frank pointed out.

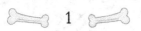

"Oh." Joe considered this. "I'm a *T. rex*, then. They're carnivores, right?"

"Right. *T. rex* loves meat. Except they didn't have hot dogs back then," Frank joked.

Joe grinned. "Ha-ha."

The two brothers had talked about nothing but dinosaurs all weekend. The next day they were going on a field trip to the Bayport Natural History Museum with their school's science club. The museum was famous for its huge brachiosaur skeleton, and a bunch of other dinosaur artifacts too. The boys couldn't wait!

Joe and Frank really liked the science club, which was led by science teacher Mr. Wachowski. Their good friends Phil Cohen and Chet Morton were in it. The other members were Tico Sanchez and Aisha Mehta from Frank's fourth-grade class and Isobel Kaltman from Joe's third-grade class. The club was pretty new, but they'd already done some cool activities—like growing bacteria in petri dishes and seeing who could turn bananas brown and yucky the fastest.

Joe took a sip of his lemonade. "Hey, Frank? What are the dinosaurs that eat everything? Om . . . Omni . . ."

"Omnivores. They eat plants *and* meat," Frank said.

"Yeah, that's me. I'm an omnivore! I'm going to hunt down hot dogs *and* french fries!" Joe reached for Frank's plate. *"Roar!"*

"Hey, those are *my* fries!" Frank protested.

Just then Aunt Gertrude strolled into the kitchen holding a basket of clean, folded laundry. "You dinosaurs need to goof around less and eat more," she scolded. "Your mother needs your help in the yard, remember?"

Joe and Frank groaned. They had almost forgotten about spring cleanup. Leave it to Aunt Gertrude to remind them of something not fun.

Still, Aunt Gertrude wasn't *always* the Queen of Chores. And she had been a big help to Mr. and Mrs. Hardy since moving in with them. She lived in a big room over the garage that Mr. Hardy had fixed up.

"Afterward can we go over to Chet's house?" Frank pleaded. "He invited us to come over and check out his new Dinosaur Rampage video game."

"Yes. Did you make up your beds?" Aunt Gertrude asked.

"Uh . . ." Joe and Frank exchanged a glance.

 4

"Yard work, then make your beds, and then you may go," Aunt Gertrude said.

The brothers nodded and quickly scarfed down the rest of their lunches.

When they had finished, they put their plates and cups in the dishwasher and headed outside. The early spring air was cool and smelled like wet leaves. In a shady spot near the driveway, the last mound of snow from winter had almost melted away. Squirrels bounded across the lawn.

Laura Hardy was busy raking one of the flower beds. She wiped her brow and smiled at her sons. "You're just in time. Can you start pulling up weeds and making a pile over there?" She pointed to a spot on the grass.

"Sure, Mom," Frank said.

"Where's Dad?" Joe asked.

"He had a meeting with Officer Heller," Mrs. Hardy replied. Fenton Hardy was a private

5

investigator who often worked with the Bayport Police. He used to be a member of the NYPD, a.k.a. the New York Police Department.

Like their father, Joe and Frank were detectives. They had solved more than a dozen mysteries in Bayport—everything from finding a missing dog to chasing down zombies. They weren't in the middle of a case at the moment, though. In fact, things had been unusually quiet in Bayport.

A little *too* quiet.

"You two must be very excited about your field trip tomorrow," Mrs. Hardy remarked.

"Yeah! Mr. W. said we get to do a dinosaur dig while we're there," Joe said eagerly.

"*And* we get to take home whatever we find," Frank added.

"Hey, guys!"

Joe and Frank turned. Chet was running down the sidewalk toward the Hardys' house.

"Hey, Chet! We're supposed to go to *your* house, remember?" Frank called out.

Chet stopped in their front yard. "I just heard some bad news, and I couldn't wait," he said, panting for breath.

"What news?" Joe demanded.

"It's about Adam Ackerman," Chet announced. "He just joined the science club. And he'll be going on the field trip with us tomorrow!"

2

Attacked!

Adam joined the science club? That *is* bad news," Frank agreed.

"Are you sure? Did Adam tell you?" Joe asked Chet.

Chet shook his head. "No way. I never talk to Adam unless I have to. I ran into Phil at the comic book store, and he told me. He heard it from Tico, who heard it from Mr. W."

Adam was the biggest bully at Bayport Ele-

mentary School. Like Joe, he was eight years old and a whole year younger than Frank. But Adam was bigger and meaner than any other eight- or nine-year-old they knew. He often got into trouble at school—and out of school too.

"Adam's going to ruin the field trip for us. I don't know how. But he'll find a way," Chet complained.

"We won't let him. We'll tell him he'd better behave . . . or else!" Joe said, shaking his fists.

"If we tell him to behave, he'll do the opposite," Frank warned. "I think the best plan is just to keep our heads down and keep our eyes open."

"Sounds good to me," Chet said quickly.

Joe frowned and said nothing.

Frank knew that his brother didn't believe in standing around and doing nothing. Joe was like a dinosaur: all action and zero patience.

 9

"Come on, Joe. Let's finish our chores so we can go to Chet's house and play Dinosaur Rampage," Frank suggested, trying to distract him from the Adam problem. "Chet, you want to help us?"

Chet eyed the rakes and shovels lying on the grass. "Sure. I guess yard work will be good practice for the dinosaur dig tomorrow!"

• • • •

"Welcome to the museum! I'm Maya Leone, and I'm an exhibit assistant here."

Maya hugged a clipboard to her chest and smiled at the science club kids. She wore a light green polo shirt with a picture of a stegosaurus and the letters *BNHM* on it. The letters stood for "Bayport Natural History Museum," Frank guessed.

"Today I'm going to be your guide through the wonderful world of dinosaurs," Maya continued.

"I'm new to the museum, so please bear with me!"

Frank, Joe, Chet, Phil, Tico, Aisha, and Isobel clustered together in the vast museum lobby, leaving their backpacks and lunch boxes with the coat check. Mr. Wachowski stood next to Maya, looking like a mad scientist with his wild gray hair and buggy black glasses.

Frank glanced around in awe. Dinosaur artifacts filled the marble and mahogany room. Some of the items were in cases; some were out in the open.

He noticed Adam hanging back from the rest of the group and checking out a bronze model of a pteranodon. Pteranodons were very large winged reptiles that lived in the time of the dinosaurs. Adam poked its outspread wings with his finger, even though the sign said NO TOUCHING!

Frank stared at him suspiciously. What was Mr. Troublemaker up to now?

"Today you're going to see some amazing dinosaur fossils," Maya said. "Can anyone tell me what a fossil is?"

Tico's hand shot up in the air. Aisha raised her hand at the same time.

"Fossils are animals or plants or other living things that are preserved—," Tico began.

"In stone or some other hard substance," Aisha cut in.

Tico glared at Aisha. She glared back.

"Yes, you're both right," Maya replied. "Does the *whole* animal or plant or other living thing have to be preserved in order for it to be considered a fossil?"

"No," Isobel said under her breath. She didn't raise her hand, though. Frank wondered why, since she obviously knew the answer.

"Anyone?" Maya prompted. "Well, the answer is no. Fossils can also be just *parts* of living things,

 13

like bones or teeth or claws. They can even be the *traces* of living things, like footprints." She paused for a moment and then added, "Okay, everyone. Follow me this way."

She continued talking about fossils as she led the group out of the lobby and down a long hall. They passed a gift shop, the Dino Deli, and the library.

At the end of the hall was a huge two-story room. In the middle of the room was a gigantic dinosaur skeleton. Frank couldn't believe his eyes. The skeleton was almost as big as his house!

"This is our famous brachiosaur. His name is Bruno, and he's . . . Let's see. He's approximately 150 million years old," Maya said, peeking at her clipboard. "For a long time the brachiosaur was considered the largest dinosaur that roamed the earth. It was an herbivore, which meant that it ate only plants."

"How could it get so huge just eating salad and stuff?" Chet asked.

"These guys ate a *lot* of leaves and twigs," Maya said with a grin. "Anyway, Bruno's not our only dinosaur. If you look around, you'll also see Alvin the allosaurus, April the apatosaurus, and Victor the velociraptor. We also have some other fun things too. Over there is an ornithopod footprint in a cast that you can touch. Ornithopods were small-to-medium-size herbivores that mostly ran on two feet. And near that is some fossilized dinosaur poop."

"Ewwwwww!" everyone groaned.

"I'm totally taking a picture of that," Phil said, reaching into his pocket for his cell phone. "Hey, Frank, do you know if—"

"Frank! Look out!" Joe yelled suddenly.

Frank turned—but not in time. He saw a dark flash of wings before something slammed into his face.

3

Fossil Wars

"Ow!" Frank yelled.

He fell back against Phil, and Phil dropped his phone to the ground. The entire group turned and stared at them.

Frank rubbed his cheek where the flying object had hit him. Joe reached down to pick it up.

It was a toy pteranodon. Joe remembered seeing a display of the toys in the doorway of the gift shop. This one still had the price tag on it, as well as a label that said TERRY THE PTERANODON.

"What on earth is going on?" Mr. Wachowski demanded. "Who threw the pteranodon at Frank? And whose cell phone is that?"

"It's mine," Phil confessed as he bent down to get it. He turned it over in the palm of his hand. "Oh, whew! The screen's not broken."

Mr. Wachowski frowned. "Let's keep our phones put away, shall we? And what about the pteranodon? Who's responsible for that?"

Someone cracked up. Joe turned around. It was Adam.

Of course.

Mr. Wachowski crossed his arms over his chest. "Adam? Do you have something you'd like to share with the rest of us?"

Adam blinked. "Who, me?" he said innocently.

"Yes, you," Mr. Wachowski replied. "Did you throw the pteranodon at Frank?"

"I was, uh, just seeing how far it could fly," Adam explained. "It was a science experiment. Frank's face got in the way."

"Does the pteranodon belong to you?" Mr. Wachowski asked him.

Adam shrugged. "I, uh, borrowed it from the gift shop. I was going to give it right back."

"Please do that. Now. And no more shenanigans from you, young man, or I'll have to call your parents to come pick you up," Mr. Wachowski warned him.

Joe handed the pteranodon to Adam. As Adam grabbed it, he bumped against Joe with his elbow— *hard*. "Sorry. Did I hurt you?" Adam taunted in a low voice.

Joe narrowed his eyes at Adam. He was *this close* to elbowing him back. Instead he took a deep breath and turned away.

After Adam left the room to return the pteranodon, Chet walked up to Joe and Frank. "I told you Adam was going to be trouble," he murmured.

"You were right," Frank said grimly. "I'm glad Mr. W. chewed him out. Maybe he'll stop being such a jerk now."

Later in the morning Maya led the group upstairs to the Young Scientists' Wing. In the center of the wing was a big, shallow pit filled with lots and lots of sand.

"A sandbox? Is this a room for babies or what?" Adam snapped.

"Actually, this is our version of a dinosaur dig site," Maya explained patiently. "Does anyone know what you call a scientist who studies dinosaurs?"

"A paleontologist," Isobel said under her breath.

"Paleontologist!" Tico and Aisha shouted at the same time.

"That's right, a paleontologist," Maya said. "Paleontologists go through dig sites around the world in search of bones, teeth, claws, eggs, and other fossils. That's what you guys are going to do here today."

Joe turned to Isobel. "You should talk louder so Maya can hear you," he advised.

Isobel blushed and shook her head quickly.

Joe didn't know Isobel very well. She was the new girl in his class. *She must be really shy,* he thought.

"You can all grab a tray and some tools from the bin over there," Maya said, pointing. "On the wall you'll see some pictures of the kinds of fossils you may come across in the sandpit. Everyone gets to take home one item they find." Then she added, "Just so you know, these aren't *real* fossils. But they're exact copies, made from liquid rubber and fiberglass. The real ones are supervaluable. They can cost hundreds or thousands of dollars, or even more."

"Whoa, that's *expensive*," Phil said.

Tico and Aisha raced over to the bin. "I call dibs!" Tico said, grabbing a fistful of tools.

"Hey, no fair. You took, like, half that stuff!" Aisha complained.

"Tico! Aisha! Let's calm down. Tico, please leave some tools for the rest of us," Mr. Wachowski said sternly.

Everyone took a tray and some tools and began digging. Joe kneeled down by the pit and sifted through the sand. After a couple of minutes he came up with . . . sand. There were no bones, teeth, claws, or other fossils in his spot.

 23

He continued digging. He still came up with nothing. Being a paleontologist was hard work!

Maya's cell phone rang. She spoke to someone briefly and hung up. "I'm so sorry, but I have to take care of something in the front office," she announced to the group. "I'll meet you all at noon in the cafeteria. In the meantime, if you find something during your dig, you can put it in one of the cloth bags that say 'Fossils-to-Go' on

them. The bag is yours to take home too. Happy hunting!"

The group continued digging. Mr. Wachowski joined in too. After a while some of the kids found bone fragments and other fossils. They stored their treasures in the Fossils-to-Go bags, just like Maya had told them to do.

"Hey, everyone! Look what I got!" Tico exclaimed. He held up a curved brown tooth. It was almost as long as his hand.

"Wait, that's *mine*! You're a thief, Tico!" Aisha cried out.

4

The Missing Tooth

Give it back!" Aisha yelled at Tico, reaching for the dinosaur tooth.

"It's mine!"

"No, it's *mine*!"

Mr. Wachowski marched up to the two of them. "What's going on? Who does this belong to?"

"It's mine. I got it first!" Tico declared.

"No, it's mine. I *saw* it first!" Aisha corrected him.

"The tooth was sticking out of the sand over there," Tico said, pointing. "I don't care if she saw

it first. She didn't call dibs or anything. I grabbed it before she did."

Mr. Wachowski turned to Aisha. "Is this true?"

"Well, yeah. Kind of. But I saw it first, and that's what counts!" Aisha insisted.

"It sounds like Tico got to it before you did," Mr. Wachowski told Aisha. "Why don't you keep digging? I'm sure you'll find something else."

"Not fair," Aisha muttered.

Tico grinned smugly and put the dinosaur tooth in one of the cloth bags, setting it aside until he could get his bag.

"Aisha doesn't look too happy," Joe whispered to Frank.

Frank nodded. "Yeah. She and Tico are competitive with each other. I wonder what's up with that."

The next day, after school, the science club met in Mr. Wachowski's classroom. Frank had always

loved Mr. W.'s room. Microscopes, beakers, and Bunsen burners covered a big table in the middle. A blue-tongued skink, which was a special kind of lizard, lived in a hundred-gallon aquarium by the windows; his name was Slither. A human skeleton occupied a back corner of the room, wearing a Bayport Bandits baseball cap.

Frank, Joe, and the other science club members had brought in their dinosaur dig fossils for a show-and-tell. "Okay, who wants to go first?" Mr. Wachowski called out. "I'm very excited to see all your discoveries."

Isobel raised her hand. "I'm sorry, Mr. Wachowski. But I, um, left my fossil at home," she apologized.

"No worries, Isobel. Just bring it in next time," Mr. Wachowski said. "Anyone else?"

Chet reached into his Fossils-to-Go bag. He held up a small, pointy fossil. "I think it might be a *T. rex* claw!" he said excitedly.

"Yeah, in your dreams. It's probably an old toothpick," Adam said, smirking.

"Adam, if you're going to be part of this group, you need to get along," Mr. Wachowski warned him.

"Fine," Adam said, rolling his eyes.

After Chet's turn Frank shared his fossil, which was a thick white bone fragment. Some of the other kids guessed that it might be a piece of a dinosaur skull. Then Joe shared his fossil, which looked like a smooth, round rock. Mr. Wachowski suggested that it might be something called a "gizzard stone." He said that some herbivores swallowed these to help them digest their food.

Tico waved his hand in the air. "Can I go next? *Please?* I really want to share my super-awesome dinosaur tooth!"

"Go ahead, Tico," Mr. Wachowski said.

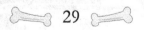

Across from Frank, Aisha rolled her eyes. *She's probably still mad at Tico,* Frank thought.

Tico dug into his backpack and pulled out his Fossils-to-Go bag. He shook it onto the table.

A fossil tumbled out. Frank frowned. It wasn't the curved brown tooth Tico had found the day

before. It was wider, flatter, and lighter in color. It had a jagged edge, like it was a fragment of something.

Alarmed, Tico stuck his hand back into the bag and said, "Hey! That's not what I was going to show. My super-awesome dinosaur tooth is gone!"

5

On the Case

Tico turned his bag inside out. There was nothing else in the bag. He searched the rest of his backpack, too. But the tooth wasn't there, either.

"Who stole my tooth fossil and left me with this dumb bone?" he called out angrily.

Isobel leaned over and peered closely at Tico's fossil. Her brown eyes widened in surprise. "It's not a dumb bone. It's a piece of a stegosaurus plate," she said slowly.

"A plate? You mean like the kind you eat on?" Phil asked, puzzled.

Isobel shook her head. "No. Stegosauruses have those big flat triangle things that stick up on their spines. They're called plates. The plates helped the stegosauruses cool off their bodies. They may have helped them scare away their enemies, too."

"Wow! How do you know so much about dinosaurs, Isobel?" Joe asked curiously.

Isobel didn't answer. She picked up Tico's fossil and turned it over in her hand. She seemed confused about something.

"I don't care if it's a stegosaurus teacup. It's not mine," Tico complained. "Who took my dinosaur tooth? Come on. Fess up! Now!"

"Nobody has your stupid tooth," Aisha snapped.

Tico grabbed Aisha's bag from her. "You took it, didn't you?"

Aisha grabbed the bag back from him. "No!

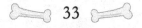 33

The only thing that's in here is my dinosaur skin fossil. Which *I* found. It's mine. See?" She dumped the contents of her bag onto the table. A strawberry-size fossil fell out. Joe stared at it. Its surface had an interesting pattern, like alligator scales.

"I'm sure your tooth will turn up," Mr. Wachowski reassured Tico.

Tico slumped down on his stool. He didn't look sure at all.

After the science club meeting was over, Tico came up to Frank and Joe in the hallway. "You guys are detectives, right? Can you find my dinosaur tooth for me? *Please?*" he begged.

Frank and Joe exchanged a glance. "Yeah, we can help you," Joe replied.

"When was the last time you saw your fossil?" Frank asked Tico.

 34

Tico considered this. "Um . . . yesterday at the museum? I put my bag in my backpack. My Fossils-to-Go bag, I mean. When I got home, we had a party for my dad's birthday, and today was school, so I didn't take the bag out till just now."

"Okay. We'll get right on your case and give you an update tomorrow," Joe promised.

"Thanks, guys!" Tico said gratefully. "If you find my tooth, I'll give you one of my super-rare editions of *Dirk Danger, Dinosaur Detective*." Among other things, Tico was a huge fan of comic books.

The Hardys said good-bye to Tico and headed home. The school was only a few blocks from their house, so they were allowed to walk on their own. Along the way they jumped over mud puddles and hummed the *Dirk Danger, Dinosaur Detective* theme—one of their favorite TV shows.

Once home, Joe and Frank said a quick hi to their mom, who was making tacos for dinner. Then they went straight to their secret tree house.

The tree house was nestled deep in the woods at the back of the Hardys' property. Their dad had built it for them. Besides their parents and Aunt Gertrude, only their closest friends even knew it existed. In fact, it was pretty much invisible unless someone was looking for it.

Joe reached up and tugged on a rope that was attached to a pulley. A second later a ladder tumbled down. He and Frank climbed up the ladder and into the tree house. They tried to be careful not to track mud on the wooden floor.

Joe set his backpack down. Frank did the same and went over to the whiteboard hanging on the wall. He picked up a pen and began to write:

WHO

WHAT

WHEN

WHERE

WHY

HOW

The boys used this note-taking method with every case. They called it the six *W*s, even though "How" wasn't a *W* word. Joe wasn't a huge fan of taking notes, but he had to admit that it helped them organize their thoughts.

"Well? Which *W* do you want to tackle first?" Frank asked Joe.

"We already know the What. Tico's dinosaur tooth is missing," Joe replied.

Frank jotted that down. "And the When is sometime yesterday or today," Frank added. He wrote: *Monday or Tuesday.*

"Now we just need the Who, Where, Why, and How," Joe said.

"The Where could be the museum or Tico's house or school—or anywhere in between," Frank guessed.

Joe nodded, thinking. A bus had taken the

science club members back to school around three o'clock yesterday. Joe didn't remember Tico or any of the other kids entering the school building before going home.

According to Tico, he'd put his Fossils-to-Go bag in his backpack at the museum and hadn't looked inside it until the science club meeting today. So Frank was right. The fossil could have disappeared at the museum, at Tico's house, at school, or anywhere in between.

Frank tapped his pen against the whiteboard. "Okay. Now let's think about the Why. Why would someone steal Tico's fossil?" he mused.

"Because someone really, really wanted it?" Joe replied.

The two brothers stared at each other and grinned. "Aisha!" they said at the same time.

6

The Suspect

The next day at recess Frank and Joe found Aisha on the playground, swinging on the yellow climbing hoops. Nearby, a bunch of kids were playing tag. Another group was digging for worms under the old maple tree.

"Hey, Aisha, can we talk to you?" Frank called out.

"What do you want? I'm kind of busy," Aisha replied, continuing to swing.

"We wanted to talk to you about Tico's dinosaur tooth," Joe said.

Aisha stopped swinging and jumped nimbly to the ground. She brushed her hands against her jeans. "What about it?" she asked suspiciously.

"He asked us to try to find it for him," Frank began.

"Why would I know anything about it? Tico lost it. It's his own fault," Aisha huffed.

"Are you sure? Because yesterday at the museum you and Tico had a big, huge fight about it," Joe reminded her. "You told everybody that it was yours. You even called him a thief."

Aisha's hazel eyes grew huge. "Wait, are you calling *me* a thief? You think *I* stole it from *him*?" she demanded.

"Well, did you?" Frank asked.

Aisha sighed. "Um, no? Even though that fossil *was* mine. I saw it first. But Tico pushed me aside and grabbed it!"

"Tico pushed you?" Joe said, surprised.

"Well, not pushed me, exactly. But you know what I mean," Aisha replied.

Frank considered this. "Why don't you and Tico like each other?" he asked after a moment.

Aisha's cheeks turned bright red. "Last week I

heard him say to a bunch of kids that he was the best at science in the whole fourth grade," she explained. "I went up and told him *I* was. He thinks he's so smart. Well, I'm smarter! I won the science fair last year at my old school, and I was only in third grade!"

Wow, Aisha's pretty competitive, Frank thought.

Actually, Aisha and Tico were both pretty competitive, at least when it came to science—and dinosaurs.

"Huh. So is that why you stole his fossil from him?" Joe piped up smoothly. "And why did you put that other fossil in his bag? Were you trying to confuse him?" Frank could tell that his brother was trying to trick Aisha into a confession.

But Aisha wasn't falling for Joe's act. "I already told you. I didn't steal it!" she said angrily. "I'm not talking to you guys anymore! Or ever again!"

With that, Aisha turned on her heel and ran off to join her friends.

 43

• • • •

After school Frank found Joe at his cubby, searching for something. Other kids were at their cubbies too, getting ready to go home.

"What's up?" Frank asked his brother.

"What? Oh, I can't find my Bandits cap," Joe replied distractedly. He rifled through gym socks, mismatched ski gloves, and a couple of old comic books.

"Okay, well, we should go. Aunt Gertrude wants us to help clean the garage, remember? Then we need to work on the case," Frank reminded him.

Joe stood up. "But we already solved the case. Aisha was lying. She stole Tico's fossil. Now we just have to make her confess and give it back to him."

Just then Tico came running down the hall. "Frank! Joe! I found my fossil!" he exclaimed.

7

A Three-Thousand-Dollar Mystery

You found your fossil?" Joe asked Tico excitedly. "Did Aisha give it back to you?"

Tico stopped in front of Joe's cubby. He frowned, confused. "What? No, not Aisha— *Adam*. I heard him talking about my fossil with Melissa and Todd," he explained.

Adam! Joe thought. *I should have known!*

"So you think Adam has it?" Frank prompted Tico.

"I *know* Adam has it. He told Melissa and Todd he owned a rare dinosaur tooth fossil. He offered to sell it to them for ten dollars," Tico replied.

"Seriously? Where is he now?" Joe asked.

"Outside," Tico replied.

"Come on. We have to stop him!" Joe said. He grabbed his backpack and started running down the hall. Frank and Tico followed.

When the three boys got outside, they found Adam standing near the idling school buses with Melissa Jones and her brother, Todd. Joe noticed that Adam was wearing a Bandits baseball cap that was several sizes too small for him. It also had a small stain on the rim.

Just like my Bandits cap, Joe thought, clenching his fists.

"Hey, Adam? Where'd you get that hat?" Joe demanded.

"I found it in some loser's cubby," Adam said, and then smirked.

"That's my hat. Give it back!" Joe fumed.

"Relax. Deep breaths," Frank whispered to Joe.

Joe was beyond trying to relax. Why did Adam have to be such a jerk all the time?

"Hey, Hardys? You're interrupting our important meeting," Melissa snapped. She pulled a small pink mirror out of her backpack and smiled at her reflection. She and Todd had been in a TV commercial once, and they thought they were celebrities—especially Melissa.

"Yeah. Melissa and Todd were about to pay me a lot of money for a very important artifat," Adam explained.

"You mean arti*fact*. And it's *my* artifact," Tico snapped.

"You mean this?" Adam held out his fist and uncurled his fingers.

Tico's dinosaur tooth!

Or was it? Joe leaned in to study it closely. On first inspection it *looked* like Tico's dinosaur tooth. It was brown and curved, and it was the right size.

But on closer inspection Joe saw that the color wasn't quite right.

He reached over and grabbed it quickly before Adam could stop him.

"Hey! That's mine! Give it back!" Adam shouted.

Joe picked up the tooth and dangled it in the air.

It was made of hard brown-colored clay.

"Looks like I just saved you guys ten dollars," Joe told Melissa and Todd.

Just then Joe noticed Isobel standing a few feet away. She was watching them intently. Joe waved to her. She blushed and quickly walked away.

Adam turned to see whom Joe had waved to. Joe took the opportunity to grab the Bandits cap off Adam's head.

"Hey!" Adam yelled.

Two for two, Joe thought triumphantly.

The next morning at breakfast Fenton Hardy set his newspaper aside and turned to his sons. "So I hear you're working on a new case," he said.

Frank nodded. "We're looking for a missing fossil."

"A fossil? Really?" Mr. Hardy said with interest.

"It's not a real fossil, exactly. It's made of liquid rubber and fiber-something," Joe replied.

"Fiberglass," Frank said.

"Yeah, that. We dug for fossils during our field trip to the Bayport Natural History Museum. Tico found a dinosaur tooth. But then someone stole it from him. Our main suspect is this girl named Aisha Mehta." Joe picked up his cereal bowl and slurped down the milk.

"Joe Hardy! Manners!" Aunt Gertrude called out from the kitchen. "And no hats at the table!"

"Sorry," Joe mumbled. He took off his Bandits cap. *Ha-ha, Adam,* he thought smugly, remembering how he had swiped the cap off Adam's head the day before.

"Wait. Did you say a dinosaur tooth? That's very odd," Mr. Hardy said.

"Why, Dad?" Frank asked curiously.

 51

Mr. Hardy picked up the newspaper and scanned the front page. "I just saw an article about a missing dinosaur tooth. Here it is."

Mr. Hardy pointed to a big headline. It read:

FOSSIL MISSING FROM NATURAL HISTORY MUSEUM

Underneath that headline, a smaller headline read:

Dinosaur Tooth Reported to Be Worth $3,000

"Three . . . thousand . . . dollars?" Joe gasped.

8

A Tale of Two Teeth

Wow, I wish my teeth were worth that much. I'd be rich!" Frank remarked.

Mr. Hardy laughed. "Very rich," he agreed.

Frank and Joe leaned in to read more. According to the article, museum officials had reported the day before that one of their dinosaur tooth fossils was missing from their collection. It was a *T. rex* tooth that paleontologists had discovered in northeastern Montana along with a lot of other

T. rex remains. The scientists believed the tooth to be approximately sixty-five million years old.

There was a photo of the lost tooth. It looked just like the tooth Tico had found on Monday.

"Wow! Tico's tooth is a *T. rex* tooth!" Joe exclaimed.

Frank frowned in confusion. Something didn't add up. "That doesn't make sense. Maya told us that the fossils we found at our dinosaur dig weren't real."

"So we're talking about *two* missing teeth? Tico's and the real one?" Joe asked.

"I don't know. We should talk to Tico about this," Frank suggested.

"We should probably visit the museum again too. Maybe Maya can tell us about the other missing tooth. The real one, I mean," Joe said.

"Good idea, Joe." Frank turned to Mr. Hardy. "Hey, Dad, can you take us to the museum after school?"

"I wish I could, but I have to meet a client. I bet Aunt Gertrude could probably drive you over, though. If you ask her nicely," Mr. Hardy said.

Aunt Gertrude popped her head out of the kitchen. "Did I hear my name? Do you boys need me to help you with your detective work?"

"Um, yes, Aunt Gertrude." Joe raised his eyebrows at Frank.

"Please," Frank added quickly.

Later that afternoon Aunt Gertrude pulled into the museum parking lot. "Here we are," she announced to Frank, Joe, and Tico, who were sitting in the backseat. "Let's go hunting for clues, or whatever it is you detectives do. I brought my flashlight and magnifying glass, just in case."

Frank had never seen their aunt so excited about anything other than housecleaning. She had been talking about fingerprints and lie detector tests during the entire ride over from school.

"I still don't get it. Why are we here?" Tico asked the brothers. "My tooth is a *pretend T. rex* tooth. The museum people are missing a *real T. rex* tooth."

"I know. But isn't it weird that your tooth and their tooth look the same? And that they both disappeared at the same time?" Frank pointed out.

"Yeah, I guess," Tico said uncertainly.

The three boys got out of the car and headed into the museum. Aunt Gertrude followed.

Frank spotted Maya near the bronze pteranodon statue in the lobby. She was talking to a man in a gray suit. A girl stood a few feet away from them, her head bent over a dog-eared book.

The girl looked familiar. Frank did a double take. It was Isobel from school!

Isobel glanced up from her book. Frank waved

57

to her. Her eyes flashed in alarm, and she looked down as though she hadn't seen the Hardys or Tico.

Frank strolled over to her. "Hey, Isobel. What are you doing here?" he asked casually.

"I—um—I'm here with my dad," Isobel stammered.

"Your dad?"

Isobel nodded toward the man in the gray suit. He was still talking to Maya.

"That's him. He's, um, a scientist," Isobel explained.

"Really? What kind of scientist?" Frank asked.

"A paleontologist," Isobel muttered under her breath.

A paleontologist?

"So *that's* why you know so much about dinosaur stuff," Frank said.

Isobel blushed. "Yeah. I didn't want anyone at school to know, though."

 58

Joe had joined them. "Why not?" he asked.

"He's kind of famous. For a paleontologist, that is," Isobel said. "At my old school they used to make fun of me and call me Baby Kaltasaurus. You know, because my last name is Kaltman. They called me other mean names too, like Dino-nerd and Geek-adon."

"That is pretty mean," Frank agreed. *That explains why she wouldn't raise her hand or answer Maya's questions during the field trip,* he thought.

"So why is your dad here?" Joe asked Isobel.

"He's a consultant for the museum. That means he helps them look at fossils and stuff and figure out what they are," Isobel replied. "He's here to talk to Maya's boss, Dr. Lebret. Dad's introducing himself to Maya now, because she's new." Then she asked, "What are you guys doing here?"

"We read about the missing *T. rex* tooth in the

newspaper. We wanted to talk to Maya about it," Joe said.

"But we're trying to help Tico find *his* missing tooth," Frank added.

Isobel dropped her book, looking flustered. She reached down to pick it up. "I'm such a klutz!" she exclaimed. "Oh, I'd better go. I think my dad's calling me. Bye. See you tomorrow at school!" She hurried away.

Frank and Joe exchanged a puzzled glance. *What was that about?* Frank wondered.

A moment later Isobel and her dad left the lobby to find Maya's boss. Maya spotted the Hardys and Tico. "Oh, hi!" she called out. "I remember you guys from Monday. Joe, Frank, and Tico, right? Are you here for another visit?"

"Actually, we're here to solve a crime. We're private investigators," Aunt Gertrude spoke up.

Maya frowned. "A . . . crime? You're . . . private investigators?"

"No! What my aunt Gertrude means is, we wanted to ask you about the missing *T. rex* tooth," Frank said quickly.

"Tico found a tooth just like it during the dinosaur dig on Monday. His tooth is missing too," Joe added.

Maya turned to Tico. "You found a *T. rex* tooth at the dinosaur dig?" she asked him sharply.

 61

Tico nodded. "Well, yeah. But mine is fake."

Maya shook her head. She seemed really upset suddenly. "You don't understand! Your tooth isn't fake. It's the real one!"

9

An Emergency Tree House Meeting

T ico's dinosaur tooth is the real one?" Joe gasped.

"The one that's worth three thousand dollars?" Frank added.

Maya nodded miserably. "Yes, I'm afraid so."

"But I found it in the sandpit! You said all the fossils in the sandpit were fake!" Tico pointed out.

"I know. I think I may have made a mistake," Maya admitted.

"What kind of mistake?" Joe asked.

Maya glanced around the lobby. A few people had just walked in and were buying tickets at the front desk. Maya gestured for Joe and the others to go over to a quiet corner of the lobby, behind a triceratops skull in a glass case.

Aunt Gertrude frowned at a fine layer of dust on the case. She pulled a lacy handkerchief out of her purse and wiped the dust away.

"I think I told you that I'm one of the exhibit assistants here," Maya began. "That means I help prepare fossils and other exhibits for display. But on Monday I was also helping to get the dinosaur dig ready for your group and for members of the general public. To do that I put a bunch of new fossils—fake fossils, that is—into the sandpit."

"I think I get it. You put a *real* fossil into the sandpit by accident," Joe said slowly.

Maya nodded. "Exactly. And when my boss finds out, she's going to kill me!"

Aunt Gertrude tapped Frank on the shoulder. "Is this where I get out my magnifying glass?" she asked in a low voice.

"Not yet, Aunt Gertrude," Frank told her. "So now all we have to do is find Tico's fossil. Then we'll solve *two* mysteries," he said to everyone else.

"Which means our case just got easier and harder at the same time," Joe remarked.

As soon as Joe and Frank got home, they headed back to the tree house. It was time for an emergency meeting.

Joe plopped down on a beanbag chair. Frank went up to the whiteboard. They had last updated the board the day before, after talking to Aisha at recess and to Adam after school.

It read:

> WHO—Aisha or Adam
> WHAT—Tico's dinosaur tooth is missing.
> Did one of the suspects steal it? Plus,
> whoever stole it put a different fossil in
> Tico's bag.
> WHEN—Monday or Tuesday
> WHERE—The museum or Tico's house or
> school or anywhere in between
> WHY—Aisha says she saw the tooth
> first and it belongs to her. Adam is a jerk
> and a bully.
> HOW—

"Now we have to add all the stuff about Tico's tooth being a real *T. rex* tooth," Frank said. He

picked up the pen and wrote under
the word "What":

Plus, it turns out Tico's tooth
isn't fake. It's a real T. rex
tooth, and it's worth $3,000.

Joe leaned back in the beanbag
chair and studied the whiteboard.

WHO-
WHAT-
WHEN-
WHERE
WHY-
HOW-

He took off his Bandits cap, turned it around, and put it back on again. He listened to the birds chirping outside. He tried to come up with a brilliant breakthrough that would solve the case once and for all.

"We don't have anything under How yet," Joe said after a moment. "Do you think that's important?"

"*Everything's* important when we're solving a case," Frank replied.

"Okay. So let's figure out the How. Tico said the last time he saw his fossil was when he put it in one of those Fossils-to-Go bags at the museum," Joe recalled.

Frank nodded. "He said he put the bag inside his backpack and didn't look at it again until the science club meeting on Tuesday."

"So someone could have taken the fossil out of his bag whenever, then put the other fossil inside.

The stegosaurus thing. What did Isobel say it was?" Joe asked.

"She said it was a piece of a stegosaurus plate," Frank replied.

"I still don't know why someone would switch fossils. To confuse Tico?" Joe wondered out loud.

Frank's brown eyes flashed. Joe knew that look. It meant that Frank was about to have a brilliant breakthrough.

"What is it?" Joe asked his brother eagerly.

"What you said just gave me an idea. What if someone didn't steal Tico's fossil?" Frank suggested.

Joe frowned. "Huh?"

"The Fossils-to-Go bags are all the same, right? What if someone mixed up his bag—or her bag— with Tico's bag by accident?" Frank said excitedly.

Joe considered this. "That makes sense. But who?"

"Joe! Frank!"

 69

Aunt Gertrude was calling to them. Joe and Frank poked their heads out the tree house door. Their aunt was down below, waving a piece of paper in the air.

"What is it, Aunt Gertrude?" Frank called down.

"I forgot to tell you. When we were in the museum, I found this clue," Aunt Gertrude explained.

The boys lowered the rope ladder and hurried down. They took the piece of paper from Aunt Gertrude and studied it.

It was an article from that morning's newspaper—the article about the missing *T. rex* tooth.

"I think it fell out of that girl's book when she dropped it," Aunt Gertrude explained.

"What girl?" Joe asked.

"That girl you were talking to, with the long brown hair," Aunt Gertrude replied.

Joe and Frank turned to each other. *Isobel!*

"Isobel didn't have a fossil on Tuesday for show-and-tell," Frank said slowly.

"That's because *her* fossil was in Tico's backpack. The stegosaurus plate," Joe added.

"Which means that she has the *T. rex* tooth!" Frank concluded.

10

Another Dinosaur Dig

Frank was excited. They'd solved the case! Frank remembered how confused Isobel had seemed at the science club meeting on Tuesday when Tico had found the stegosaurus plate in his bag. It all made sense now, since that had been *her* stegosaurus plate.

Except . . . if Isobel had figured out that she'd taken Tico's fossil by mistake, why hadn't she come forward? Especially when she'd realized that Tico's "fake" *T. rex* tooth was actually the *real T. rex* tooth that was missing from the museum?

"Great detective work, Aunt Gertrude," Joe told her.

Aunt Gertrude flushed with pleasure. "Thank you!"

"Do we have time to stop by Isobel's house before dinner?" Frank asked her. "We really need to talk to her."

Aunt Gertrude glanced at her watch. "Well . . . maybe I could keep the lasagna warm in the oven. I'll let your parents know. Do you need a ride?"

"Yes!" Joe said.

"Please!" Frank added.

"I'll get my keys. And, boys? Please change your shoes before we leave. You can't go over to someone's house in those dirty, disgusting sneakers," Aunt Gertrude said sternly.

Frank and Joe smiled at each other. Aunt Gertrude was still Aunt Gertrude, detective or not!

Fifteen minutes later Frank and Joe stood on Isobel's front porch and rang the bell. They had called Maya at the museum and gotten the Kaltmans' address from her. Aunt Gertrude waited for the boys in the car.

The Kaltmans' house was a big, rambling gray Victorian that backed up onto Bayport Park. A metal sculpture of a *T. rex* decorated the front yard. Rolled-up maps and what looked like digging tools covered the front porch.

Inside the house a dog began barking. Then Isobel opened the door. She frowned when she saw the Hardys standing there.

"How . . . I mean, what are you doing here?" Isobel asked nervously. "Shhh, Poppy," she scolded her dog, who was still barking.

"We want to talk to you about Tico's *T. rex* tooth. The museum's *T. rex* tooth, I mean," Frank explained.

"We know you have it, Isobel," Joe blurted out. "You switched Tico's bag with your bag by accident, didn't you? Or did you do it on purpose?"

Isobel startled.

She glanced over her shoulder and stepped outside. Poppy followed, baring her teeth and growling at the Hardys. Isobel closed the door behind them.

"It's okay, Poppy. They're from my school," Isobel told the dog. Poppy whimpered and lay down at her feet.

"I didn't do it on purpose. It was an accident. I would never steal someone else's things," Isobel told Frank and Joe. "I didn't realize I had the wrong fossil until Tuesday. Not until we did show-and-tell during science club."

"So where is it? Where's the tooth?" Frank asked her.

"I have no idea," Isobel confessed.

"What do you mean, you have no idea?" Joe demanded.

Isobel sighed. "After I got home from the field trip on Monday, I put my backpack in my room. My Fossils-to-Go bag was inside it. That is, it was Tico's fossil bag, but I didn't know that at the time," she corrected herself quickly. "Well, Poppy got into my backpack while I was helping with dinner. I think he pulled the *T. rex* tooth out and buried it in the yard. He's done stuff like that before. Until show-and-tell on Tuesday, I thought Poppy had just taken my fake stegosaurus fossil."

"Poppy buried a real three-thousand-dollar fossil?" Frank gasped.

Poppy looked at Frank with guilty eyes.

"I've been looking everywhere for it, but I can't find it," Isobel moaned. "I know I should tell my parents and Mr. Wachowski—and the museum people too. I'm going to be in *so* much trouble."

"Hmm. Maybe we can help you find it now," Frank suggested.

Joe nodded. "Yeah. Maybe we can have another dinosaur dig—in your yard!"

 77

Isobel's face lit up. "Okay, if you think it'll work. Here. We can borrow some of my dad's tools."

The three kids picked out some shovels and rakes from the pile of digging tools. Isobel led them to the backyard. "This is where Poppy usually buries her treasures," she said, waving her arm in a wide arc.

Frank glanced around the yard. The back of it bordered on Bayport Park. What if Poppy had buried the fossil in the park instead of the yard? They would never find it then.

Then something occurred to Frank.

"Hey, I have an idea. Can you go get your Fossils-to-Go bag?" he asked Isobel.

"Sure," Isobel said.

She went inside her house, Poppy at her heels. The two of them returned a few minutes later with the bag.

78

Frank took the bag from Isobel and held it out to Poppy. Poppy sniffed it eagerly.

"Go fetch, Poppy," Frank commanded the dog. "Where'd you bury it? Where'd you bury the dinosaur tooth?"

Poppy barked excitedly. Then he took off running.

Frank, Joe, and Isobel followed, carrying their tools. Poppy stopped at the base of a tall oak tree and began digging frantically.

Poppy dug . . . and dug . . . and dug. He bent down and gripped something with his teeth. Was it the tooth?

No. It was a red ball.

"False alarm," Frank announced, biting back his disappointment.

"Wait a second." Joe pushed his shovel into the dirt where Poppy had been digging. He upturned a big mound of dirt.

 79

Joe sifted through the dirt. There was a raw-hide bone. And a football-shaped chew toy. And an old sock.

Under the old sock was the *T. rex* tooth!

Joe picked it up and cleaned the dirt off with the hem of his shirt. It was definitely the missing tooth.

"Yay, we found it!" Joe announced.

"Yay!" Isobel shouted happily.

The three kids high-fived. Poppy began barking again.

On Saturday morning Frank and Joe took their breakfast up to the tree house. They both wore hoodies over their pajamas, and rain boots. They didn't want Aunt Gertrude lecturing them about muddy shoes.

Joe sat down on the beanbag chair and speared a blueberry pancake with his fork. Frank folded a pancake in half like a taco and ate it with his hands as he walked up to the whiteboard.

The notes from Thursday were still intact.

Frank picked up the pen and added Isobel's name to the Who list. Then he wrote under How:

> Isobel took Tico's bag by accident.
> It had the real T. rex tooth in it. Her
> dog, Poppy, buried the tooth in their
> backyard.

Joe reached into the pocket of his hoodie and handed something to Frank. It was an article that had appeared in that morning's newspaper. The headline read:

TWO LOCAL BOYS FIND MISSING T. REX TOOTH IN BACKYARD

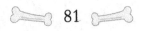

Underneath the headline was a photo of Frank and Joe.

"Don't forget to tape that up on the wall," Joe told Frank proudly.

Frank grinned. "I won't! And there's something else I need to do."

He picked up the pen again and wrote on the whiteboard:

SECRET FILES CASE #14: SOLVED!

A Dino-mite Mini Glossary

allosaurus—A type of carnivore with six-inch-long claws and very sharp teeth. It may have hunted in packs.

apatosaurus—A type of herbivore with a very long neck and whiplike tail. It was part of the sauropod group of dinosaurs, which were among the largest creatures ever to walk on land.

brachiosaur—A type of herbivore with a very long neck and small skull. Like the apatosaurus, it was part of the sauropod group of dinosaurs.

carnivore—A living organism that eats only meat.

herbivore—A living organism that eats only plants.

omnivore—A living organism that eats both plants and meat.

ornithopod—A type of dinosaur that was small-to-medium-size, mostly ran on two feet, and was herbivorous. An iguanodon is an example of a dinosaur that was in the ornithopod group.

pteranodon—A very large winged reptile that lived in the time of the dinosaurs.

sauropod—A type of herbivore with a very long neck, a long tail, a small head, and thick, pillar-like legs.

stegosaurus—A type of herbivore with spikes on its tail and rows of bony plates along its back. Scientists believe that the plates were used for cooling the stegosaurus's body and for scaring away its enemies.

triceratops—A type of herbivore with three horns and a large, bony neck frill. It had anywhere from 432–800 teeth and used them to shear its food.

Tyrannosaurus rex—A type of carnivore with tiny arms, strong back legs, and very sharp teeth.

The name is often shortened to *T. rex* and means "king of the tyrant lizards."

ultrasaurus—A type of herbivore with a very long neck, a tiny mouth, small teeth, and nostrils on the top of its head. Like the apatosaurus and brachiosaur, it was part of the sauropod group of dinosaurs.

velociraptor—A type of carnivore with very sharp claws and teeth. It was small, fast, and skilled at hunting.

Join Zeus and his friends as they set off on the adventure of a lifetime.

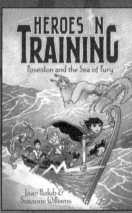

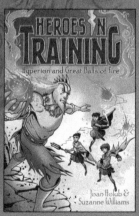

NANCY DREW AND THE CLUE CREW®

Test your detective skills with more Clue Crew cases!

FROM ALADDIN • PUBLISHED BY SIMON & SCHUSTER